MW00908700

Text copyright © year of publication by individual authors
Illustrations copyright © year of publication by individual illustrators

All rights reserved.

First U.S. edition 1996

Library of Congress Cataloging-in-Publication Data

The Candlewick book of animal tales. — 1st U.S. ed.
Summary: A collection of original and traditional stories and rhymes
about a variety of animals by different authors and illustrators.
ISBN 0-7636-0012-1
1. Animals — Literary collections. [1. Animals — Literary collections.]
PZ5.C1682   1996
808.83'936 — dc20   95-45712

2 4 6 8 10 9 7 5 3 1

Printed in Italy

Candlewick Press
2067 Massachusetts Avenue
Cambridge, Massachusetts 02140

THE CANDLEWICK BOOK OF
ANIMAL TALES

CANDLEWICK PRESS
CAMBRIDGE, MASSACHUSETTS

CONTENTS

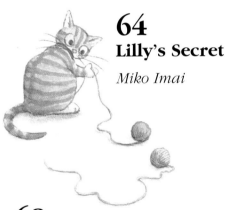

The Pig in the Pond

Martin Waddell

illustrated by **Jill Barton**

This is the story of
Neligan's pig.
One day Neligan
went into town.
It was hot. It was dry.
The sun shone in the sky.
Neligan's pig sat by
Neligan's pond.
The ducks went, "Quack!"
The geese went, "Honk!"

They were cool on
the water in
Neligan's pond.
The pig sat in the sun.
She looked at the pond.
The ducks went, "Quack!"
The geese went, "Honk!"
The pig went, "Oink!"
She didn't go in,
because pigs don't swim.

The pig sat in the sun getting hotter and hotter. The ducks went, "Quack, quack!" The geese went, "Honk, honk!" The pig went, "Oink, oink!" She didn't go in, because pigs don't swim.

The pig gulped and gasped and looked at the water. The ducks went, "Quack, quack, quack!" The geese went, "Honk, honk, honk!" The pig went, "Oink, oink, oink!"

She rose from the ground and turned around and around, stamping her feet and twirling her tail, and . . .

SPLASH! **SPLASH!** **SPLASH!** **SPLASH!** **SPLASH!**

The ducks and the geese were splashed out of the pond.

The ducks went, "Quack,
quack, quack, quack!"
The geese went, "Honk,
honk, honk, honk!" which
means, very loudly,
"The pig's in the pond!"

"The pig's in the pond!"
"The pig's in the pond!"
The word spread about,
above, and beyond,

"The pig's in the pond!"
"The pig's in the pond!"
"At Neligan's farm,
the pig's in the pond!"

From the fields all
around they came to see the
pig in the pond at Neligan's
farm. And then . . .

Neligan came on his cart!

Neligan looked at the pig in the pond.
The pig went, "Oink!"
Neligan took off his hat.

Neligan looked at the pig in the pond.
The pig went, "Oink, oink!"
Neligan took off his pants and boots.

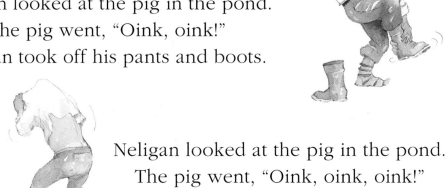

Neligan looked at the pig in the pond.
The pig went, "Oink, oink, oink!"
Neligan took off his shirt.

Neligan looked at the pig in the pond.
The pig went, "Oink, oink, oink, OINK!"
Neligan took off his underwear and . . .

SPLASH!

Neligan joined the pig in the pond. What happened next?

SPLOOOOOOOOSH!

They all joined the pig in the pond!

And that was the story of Neligan's pig.

"Have You Seen the Crocodile?"

Colin West

"Have you seen the crocodile?" asked the parrot.

"No," said the dragonfly.

"Have you seen the crocodile?" asked the parrot and the dragonfly.

"No," said the bumblebee.

"Have you seen the crocodile?"
asked the parrot
and the dragonfly
and the
bumblebee.

"No,"
said the
butterfly.

"Have you seen the crocodile?"
asked the parrot
and the dragonfly
and the bumblebee
and the butterfly.

"No,"
said the
hummingbird.

"Have you seen the crocodile?"
asked the parrot
and the dragonfly
and the bumblebee
and the butterfly
and the hummingbird.

"No,"
said the
frog.

"No one's seen the crocodile!"
said the parrot
and the dragonfly
and the bumblebee
and the butterfly
and the hummingbird
and the frog.

"I'VE SEEN THE CROCODILE!"
snapped the crocodile.

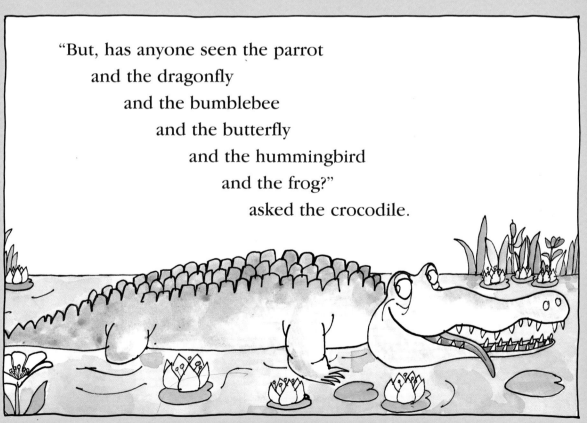

"But, has anyone seen the parrot
and the dragonfly
and the bumblebee
and the butterfly
and the hummingbird
and the frog?"
asked the crocodile.

The Hare
and the Tortoise

retold by Margaret Clark

illustrated by Charlotte Voake

A *hare was one day
making fun of a tortoise.*

"You are a slowpoke," he said. "You couldn't run if you tried."

"Don't you laugh at me," said the tortoise. "I bet that I could beat you in a race."

"Couldn't," replied the hare.

"Could," said the tortoise.

"All right," said the hare. "I'll race you. But I'll win, even with my eyes shut."

They asked a passing fox to start them off.

"Ready, set, go!" said the fox.

The hare took off at a great pace. He got so far ahead he decided he might as well stop for a rest.

Soon he fell fast asleep.

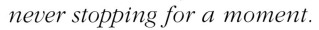

The tortoise came plodding along, never stopping for a moment.

When the hare woke up, he ran as fast as he could to the finish line . . .

But he was too late—the tortoise had already won the race!

PEBBLE GOES TO TOWN

BENEDICT BLATHWAYT

Pebble the pony lived on the moor. It was a high, wild, and lonely place. Summer was Pebble's favorite season.

Vacationers from the town came up to the moor: walkers . . . painters . . . bird watchers . . . and cyclists. But Pebble liked the picnickers best of all. He grew very fond of crusts and cake and apple peel.

Tough grass tasted dull after picnic scraps.

The town must be a wonderful place, thought Pebble. All those people! All those picnics!

Pebble made up his mind to visit the town.

One evening he set off down the hill.

By early morning, Pebble had reached the town. The streets were empty. There were no picnics here. He could smell bread and cakes, but they weren't for him—it wasn't such a wonderful place after all.

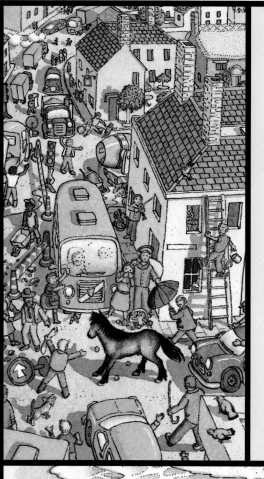

And then the town woke up and Pebble wished he were back on the moor . . . but which road would take him home?

He just had to get away, away from the noise and the smoke, anywhere would do.

Pebble was exhausted.

This was as far as he could go.

An old lady offered Pebble a cookie.

"I'm Miss Moss," she said. "I live on the moor, too. I can see you are lost. Let me take you home." She led Pebble back up the hill.

Soon Pebble could smell moorland grass and hear the running of streams.

Miss Moss set Pebble free. How wonderful it is to be home, he thought . . .

I'll never go down to town again.

You're a Hero, Daley B.!

Daley B. didn't know
what he was.
"Am I a monkey?" he said.
"Am I a koala? Am I
a porcupine?"

Daley B. didn't know
where to live.
"Should I live in a cave?"
he said. "Should I live in a
nest? Should I live in a web?"

Daley B. didn't know
what to eat.
"Should I eat fish?" he said.
"Should I eat potatoes?
Should I eat worms?"

Daley B. didn't know
why his feet were so big.
"Are they for water-skiing?"
he said. "Are they for the
mice to sit on? Are they to
keep the rain off?"

Daley B. saw the birds in
the tree and decided he
would live in a tree.

Daley B. saw the squirrels
eating acorns and decided
he would eat acorns.

But he still didn't know
why his feet were so big.

Jon Blake   illustrated by Axel Scheffler

One day there was a great
panic in the woods.
All the rabbits gathered
beneath Daley B.'s tree.
"You must come down at
once, Daley B.!" they cried.
"Jazzy D. is coming!"

"Who is Jazzy D.?"
asked Daley B.
The rabbits were too
excited to answer. They
scattered across the grass
and vanished into
their burrows.

Daley B. stayed in his tree,
nibbled another acorn, and
wondered about
his big feet.

Jazzy D. crept out of the
bushes. Her teeth were as
sharp as broken glass, and
her eyes were as quick
as fleas.

Jazzy D. sneaked around
the burrows, but there was
not a rabbit to be seen.

Jazzy D. looked up.

Daley B. waved.

Jazzy D. began to climb
the tree.

The other rabbits poked
out their noses
and trembled.

"Hello," said Daley B.
to Jazzy D. "Are
you a badger? Are
you an elephant?
Are you a
duck-billed
platypus?"

Jazzy D. crept closer. "No, my friend," she whispered. "I am a weasel."

"Do you live in a pond?" asked Daley B. "Do you live in a dam? Do you live in a kennel?"

Jazzy D. crept closer still. "No, my friend," she hissed, "I live in the darkest corner of the woods."

"Do you eat cabbages?" asked Daley B. "Do you eat insects? Do you eat fruit?"

Jazzy D. crept right up to Daley B. "No, my friend," she rasped. "I eat rabbits! Rabbits like *you*!"

Daley B.'s face fell. "Am I . . . a rabbit?" he stammered.

Jazzy D. nodded . . .

and licked her lips . . .

and leapt!

28

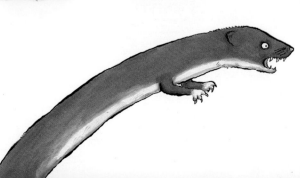

Daley B. didn't have to think.
Quick as a flash, he kicked out
with his massive feet.

Jazzy D. sailed
through the air,
far far away, back
where she came
from.

The other rabbits jumped
and cheered and hugged
each other.

"You're a hero, Daley B.!"
they cried.

"That's funny,"
said Daley B.
"I thought I was
a rabbit."

Emma's Lamb
Kim Lewis

One rainy spring morning at lambing time, Emma's father put a little lost lamb in a box by the stove. Then he went back to the field to look for Lamb's mother.

Lamb and Emma looked at each other.

"Baaa," said Lamb, sitting up in his box.

Emma wanted to keep little Lamb and

30

look after him all by
herself. So she dried
Lamb because he was
very wet. She tried to
keep him warm
because he was very
cold. Emma fed Lamb
because he was very
hungry.

When Lamb was dry
and warm and fed, he
and Emma played.

"Baaa," said Lamb.

Then Emma took Lamb for a walk and he skipped along behind her. Emma decided to play hide-and-seek.

She closed her eyes and counted to ten.

"Here I come!" she cried.

Emma looked for Lamb in the stable. She looked for him in the barn. She looked for him in the granary. She looked all around the yard.

She couldn't find Lamb in the house. He wasn't in his box. She couldn't find him in the sheep pens either.

"I give up!" she shouted.

But Lamb was nowhere to be found.

Emma didn't want to play anymore. She wanted Lamb to come back. She thought he might be cold and hungry.

"Where are you, Lamb?" she cried.

"Baaa," came a sound from the hayshed.

Emma ran inside to look. Lamb sat up in the nesting box, where the hens had laid their eggs.

"Baaa," he cried and ran to Emma.

"Lamb, I thought I'd lost you," said Emma, holding him very tight.

She couldn't look after Lamb all by herself. He needed to be with his mother.

But where was she?

Then Emma saw her father across the field. A ewe without a lamb ran ahead of him, calling.

"Baaa," cried Lamb. He wriggled to get free.

Emma put him down, and Lamb ran as fast as he could to his mother.

Emma went to the field the very next day. When she called, Lamb came running to see her.

"Will you remember me?" asked Emma.

Lamb and Emma looked at each other.

"Baaa," said Lamb, waggling his tail.

Over in the meadow
in the sand in the sun . . .
Lived an old mother turtle
and her little turtle
ONE.
"Dig," said his mother.
"I dig," said the One.
So he dug all day
in the sand in the sun.

Over in the meadow
where the stream runs blue,
Lived an old mother duck
and her little ducklings
TWO.
"Quack," said their mother.
"We quack," said the Two.
So they quacked all day
where the stream runs blue.

Over in the meadow
in a hole in a tree,
Lived an old mother owl
and her little owls
THREE.
"Who-whoo," said their mother.
"Who-whoo," said the Three;
So they who-whooed all day
in a hole in a tree.

Over in the meadow
by the big barn door,
Lived an old mother mouse
and her little mice
FOUR.
"Squeak," said their mother.
"We squeak," said the Four.
So they squeaked all day
by the big barn door.

Over in the meadow
in a snug beehive,
Lived an old mother bee
and her little bees
FIVE.
"Buzz," said their mother.
"We buzz," said the Five.
So they buzzed all day
round their snug beehive.

Over in the meadow
in a nest built of sticks,
Lived an old mother squirrel
and her little squirrels
SIX.
"Jump," said their mother.
"We jump," said the Six.
So they jumped all day
round their nest built of sticks.

Over in the meadow
where the grass grows so even,
Lived an old mother frog
and her little froggies
SEVEN.
"Hop!" said their mother.
"We hop!" said the Seven.
So they hopped all day
where the grass grows so even.

Over in the meadow
near the little mossy gate,
Lived an old mother lizard
and her little lizards
EIGHT.
"Run," said their mother.
"We run," said the Eight.
So they ran all day
on the little mossy gate.

Over in the meadow
by the tall green pine,
Lived an old mother pig
and her little piglets
NINE.
"Oink!" said their mother.
"We oink," said the Nine.
So they oinked all day
near the tall green pine.

Over in the meadow
in a cozy little den,
Lived an old mother fox
and her little foxes
TEN.
"Play," said their mother.
"We play," said the Ten.
So they played all day
round their cozy little den.

Over in the meadow in the sand in the sun . . .

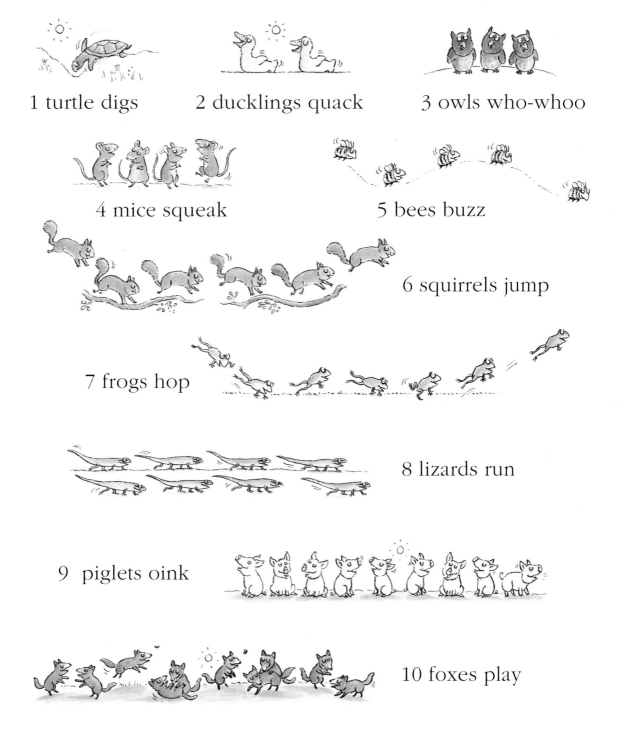

1 turtle digs 2 ducklings quack 3 owls who-whoo

4 mice squeak 5 bees buzz

6 squirrels jump

7 frogs hop

8 lizards run

9 piglets oink

10 foxes play

over in the meadow till the end of the day.

My Hen Is Dancing

Karen Wallace

illustrated by Anita Jeram

My hen is dancing in the farmyard. She takes two steps forward and one step back. She bends her neck and pecks and scratches. Her beak snaps shut. She's found a worm.

My hen is rolling in her dust bath. She likes the ground when it's gritty and dry. She cleans her feathers with her beak and scratches her ears with her toenails.

She stretches her wings and sleeps in the sun.

My hen never struggles
if you hold her.
Her feathers
are long and
smooth on
her wings.

Underneath she's soft
like a feather duster.
Her bones
feel hard like
thin sticks
inside her.

43

My hen lives in a henhouse with five other hens. There's fresh straw on the floor and a row of nest boxes along the back wall.

A rooster lives there too. He has shiny tail feathers and a red coxcomb like a crown. If my hen wanders, he brings her home.

My hen lays big brown eggs. When there are chicks growing inside them, she sits in her nest box and puffs up her feathers. She pecks you if you try to touch them. Her chicks are wet and sticky when they hatch.

She sleeps standing up. Her long toes grip the perch so she doesn't fall.

They creep underneath her where she's fluffy and warm.

My hen leads her chicks around the farmyard. They learn to scratch and peck and pull worms from the ground.

My hen knows when it's time to.go to sleep. As soon as it gets dark, she hops into the henhouse.

We close the henhouse door at night to keep her safe from hungry foxes.

In the morning I open the door. The rooster jumps out with my hen close behind him. The rooster crows, and she steps up beside him.

My hen is dancing in the farmyard.

Little Beaver and the Echo

Amy MacDonald
illustrated by Sarah Fox-Davies

Little Beaver lived all alone by the edge of a big pond. He didn't have any brothers. He didn't have any sisters. Worst of all, he didn't have any friends. One day, sitting by the side of the pond, he began to cry. He cried out loud. Then he cried out louder.

Suddenly, he heard something very strange. On the other side of the pond, someone else was crying too. Little Beaver stopped crying and listened. The other crying stopped. Little Beaver was alone again.

"Booo hooo," he said.

"Booo hooo," said the voice from across the pond.

"Huh-huh-waaah!" said Little Beaver.

"Huh-huh-waaah!" said the voice from across the pond.

Little Beaver stopped crying. "Hello!" he called.

"Hello!" said the voice from across the pond.

"Why are you crying?" asked Little Beaver.

"Why are you crying?" asked the voice from across the pond.

Little Beaver thought for a moment. "I'm lonely," he said. "I need a friend."

"I'm lonely," said the voice from across the pond. "I need a friend."

Little Beaver couldn't believe it. On the other side of the pond lived somebody else who was sad and needed a friend. He got right into his boat and set off to find him.

It was a big pond. He paddled and paddled. Then he saw a young duck, swimming in circles all by himself.

"I'm looking for someone who needs a friend," said Little Beaver. "Was it *you* who was crying?"

"I do need a friend," said the duck. "But it wasn't me who was crying."

"I'll be your friend," said Little Beaver. "Come with me."

So the duck jumped into the boat.

They paddled and paddled. Then they saw a young otter, sliding up and down the bank all by himself.

"We're looking for someone who needs a friend," said Little Beaver. "Was it *you* who was crying?"

"I do need a friend," said the otter. "But it wasn't me who was crying."

"We'll be your friends," said Little Beaver and the duck. "Come with us."

So the otter jumped into the boat.

They paddled and paddled. Then they saw a young turtle, sunning himself all alone on a rock.

"We're looking for someone who needs a friend," said Little Beaver. "Was it *you* who was crying?"

"I do need a friend," said the turtle. "But it wasn't me who was crying."

"We'll be your friends," said Little Beaver and the duck and the otter. "Come with us."

So the turtle jumped into the boat, and they paddled and paddled until they came to the end of the pond.

Here lived a wise old beaver, in a mud house, all alone. Little Beaver told him how they had paddled all around the pond, to find out who was crying.

"It wasn't the duck," he said. "It wasn't the otter. And it wasn't the turtle. Who was it?"

"It was the Echo," said the wise old beaver.

"Where does he live?" asked Little Beaver.

"On the other side of the pond," said the wise old beaver. "No matter where you are, the Echo is always across the pond from you."

"Why is he crying?" said Little Beaver.

"When you are sad, the Echo is sad," said the wise old beaver. "When you are happy, the Echo is happy too."

"But how can I find him and be his friend?" asked Little Beaver. "He doesn't have any friends, and neither do I."

"Except for me," said the duck.

"And me," said the otter.

"And me," said the turtle.

Little Beaver looked surprised. "Yes," he said. "I have lots of friends now!"

And he was so happy that he said it again, very loudly: "I have lots of friends now!"

From across the pond, a voice answered him: "I have lots of friends now!"

"You see?" said the wise old beaver. "When you're happy, the Echo is happy. When you have friends, he has friends too."

"Hooray!" shouted Little Beaver and the duck and the otter and the turtle, all together.

And the Echo shouted back to them: "Hooray!"

BREAKFAST ON ROSIE'S FARM

Zita Newcome

This is Rosie.
She lives on a farm.

Every morning Rosie gets up early when the sun rises.
She puts on her clothes and hurries outside to
feed the hens.

Then she feeds the pigs
a bucket of old potatoes.

She rubs noses with Daisy the cow.

Rosie visits the sheep next and gives a baby
lamb a bottle of milk.

Then Rosie gives the horse an apple.

Back inside Rosie's house,
the dogs are waiting for their breakfast.

The goldfish are also hungry and need to be fed.

The cat would like milk in her bowl.

Then, finally, Rosie can eat her own breakfast.

ALONG CAME TOTO

Anni Axworthy

This is Percy, who lived very happily in a house that was all his own.

Then one day a brown box came, and out of the box came **Toto.**

Percy went to
play with his toys.

Along came Toto.

Percy went to
eat his dinner.

Along came Toto.

Percy went out
in the garden.

Along came Toto.

Whatever Percy
did and wherever
Percy went,

along came Toto.

Percy got grumbly and growly
and grouchy. He grumped
upstairs to bed.

Along came Toto.

"Go away!" roared Percy.
"You fiddly flea! You
measly monkey!
You teeny-tiny,
teensy-weensy,
tiddly-widdly
TIGER!
I just
want to
sleep on
my own!"

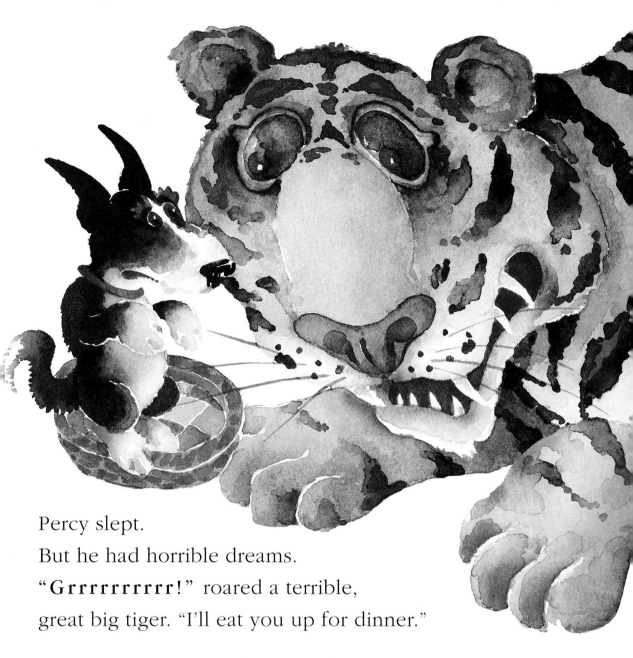

Percy slept.

But he had horrible dreams.

"**Grrrrrrrrrr!**" roared a terrible,
great big tiger. "I'll eat you up for dinner."

Percy woke up.

"**Prrrrrrrr!**" Something
small and soft and
warm was purring in
Percy's basket.
"Oh, Toto," Percy
said, "I'm glad you
came along."

Sam Vole

and His Brothers

Martin Waddell

illustrated by Barbara Firth

S am Vole had big brothers, Arthur and Henry. Sam wanted to do things all by himself, but wherever he went his brothers went too.

"I'm going voling for nuts," Sam told Mother. "I'm going voling all by myself."

Sam went voling out in the meadow, but Arthur and Henry went too.

They brought home more nuts than Sam, enough for them all. Sam gave his nuts to Mother.

"I'm going voling for grass," Sam told Mother. "I'm going voling all by myself."

Sam went voling out in the meadow, but Arthur and Henry went too.

They carried home more grass than Sam, enough for them all. Sam gave his grass to Mother.

"I'm going voling for daisies," Sam told Mother. "I'm going voling all by myself."

Sam went voling out in the meadow, but Arthur and Henry went too.

They picked more daisies than Sam, enough for them all. Sam gave his daisies to Mother.

When they all went to bed, Sam could not sleep. He lay awake thinking, *I want to do something all by myself.*

Early next morning he did it. He slipped out of the house and into the meadow, and he went voling alone.

He voled and he voled all by himself and he sang and he danced, for he liked it so much without brothers.

He voled and he voled all by himself and he walked and he whistled, for he still liked it a little without brothers.

He voled and he voled all by himself.

Then he stopped and he stood and he listened.

He voled and he voled all by himself and he ran and he jumped, for he liked it a lot without brothers.

He didn't like it at all without brothers.
Sam sat and felt sad without brothers.

Then he saw . . .

Arthur and Henry, his brothers.

And Sam said, "I've been voling alone
all by myself. Now I'll vole with you.
You're my brothers."

And they voled around
the meadow together.
And then . . .

the brothers voled
happily home.

Lilly's Secret

Miko Imai

Lilly was a little cat who lived in a little house in a little town.

One afternoon she was having tea when her new neighbor Coco stopped by and helped herself to a mouse biscuit.

"So, Lilly, did I see you with Joey last night?"

"Yes," said Lilly. "We went for a walk."

"Oh *really*?" said Coco. "Has he noticed your funny paws? They're so weird!"

Coco grabbed the last biscuit and left.

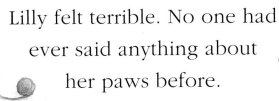

Lilly felt terrible. No one had
ever said anything about
her paws before.

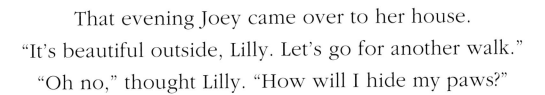

Suddenly they seemed really big
and ugly. She wanted to cover
them up. But nothing
seemed to work.

That evening Joey came over to her house.
"It's beautiful outside, Lilly. Let's go for another walk."
"Oh no," thought Lilly. "How will I hide my paws?"

"Hi, Joey,"
she said shyly.
"Hello, Lilly.
Don't you want
to hold my paw
tonight?"
Lilly didn't
know what to
say. She shook
her head sadly.

Then she
saw Coco.
"Hi, Lilly."
Lilly was
sure Coco
had told the other
cats her secret.
What if she told Joey
too? Lilly couldn't
stand it anymore!

She ran and she ran
as fast as she could.
"What's the matter?"
Joey asked.
"Coco was going to
tell you about my paws.
She said they were weird.
I didn't want you to know about them."
"Don't be silly, Lilly! I've always known about
your funny paws. I like them."

"Besides, you never said anything
about my crooked tail!"

MOLES CAN DANCE

Richard Edwards • illustrated by Caroline Anstey

In the warm wormy darkness underground, moles were doing their work. All day long they dug tunnels and corridors and pushed up molehills into the field above. It was tiring work, and the young mole soon got bored.

"I'm worn out," he said, "and I'm all cramped up, I don't like digging. I want to stretch. I want to run around. I want to . . . *dance!*"

"Moles can't dance," said the old mole. "Moles aren't made for dancing—they're made for digging. Whoever heard of a mole dancing!"

"Moles can't dance," said all the other moles.

"See," said the old mole. "What did I tell you? Now stop being silly and dig that tunnel."

The young mole dug as he was told, but all the time he was thinking: I want to learn to dance. Why shouldn't I learn to dance? It's not fair.

Then he had an idea. If the moles couldn't teach him to dance, perhaps someone else could. Quickly he scrabbled his way upward and broke out into the dazzling sunshine of the field.

A cow was looking at him.

"I want to learn to dance," said the young mole.

"I can't teach you," said the cow. "Cows can't dance. They can chew grass and wave their tails and moo, but they can't dance."

And it went on chewing grass.

The mole walked on and met a frog.

"I want to learn to dance," said the mole.

"I can't teach you," said the frog. "Frogs can't dance. They can hop around and swim, but they can't dance."

And it hopped into the pond and swam away.

Next, the mole met a fox.

"I want to learn to dance," said the mole.

"I can't teach you," said the fox. "Foxes can't dance. They can prowl around the fields, keeping very quiet, but they can't dance."

And it went on prowling.

The mole walked on and saw a woodpecker hammering at a tree.

"I want to learn to dance," called the mole.

"I can't teach you," said the woodpecker. "Woodpeckers can't dance. They can fly from tree to tree, bashing the bark with their beaks, but they can't dance."

And it went on bashing.

Then the mole heard a funny noise coming from behind a hedge.

THUMPA THUMPA THUMPA

What could it be?

THUMPA THUMPA THUMPA

The mole crawled into the hedge and looked out on the other side.

Two children were playing in a garden. Dodge was making the *THUMPA THUMPA THUMPA* by banging on some boxes, and Daisy was dancing on the grass.

Real dancing! The mole had never seen anything so fine in all his life.

Dodge drummed and Daisy danced and the mole watched carefully.

Daisy spun around on one leg, and the mole spun around on one leg.

Daisy did a cartwheel, and the mole did a cartwheel.

Daisy hopped up and down, and so did the mole.

Every step that Daisy danced, the mole danced too, until shadows began to creep across the garden.

"Better get back," said the mole to himself. "It's getting late." And he turned and began to dance his way home.

The woodpecker was so surprised to see the mole dancing back along the path that it almost fell off its branch.

The fox was so surprised to see the mole dancing along the hedgerow that it almost toppled into a ditch.

The frog was so surprised to see the mole dancing past the pond that it swallowed a mouthful of muddy water.

The cow was so surprised to see the mole dancing across the field that it stood still for a long time, with a grass stalk sticking out of its mouth.

"Where have you been?" asked the old mole.

"Just . . . dancing," said the young mole.

"Moles can't dance," said the old mole.

"Oh, yes they can," said the young mole. "I'll show you." And he climbed on to the top of the nearest molehill and began to hop and spin around.

Soon all the other moles came up to see what was happening.

"He's dancing!" said one mole. "And if he can, so can we. Come on!"

So, in ones and twos and threes, they all began to dance—some on molehills, some on the grass, some very badly, some very well, some moles hopping, some moles jumping and some moles spinning around, but all of them, even the old mole, having a fine time as they danced and danced and danced and danced by the light of the climbing moon.

POLAR BEAR CAT

If I were a polar bear
instead of a cat,

I would slide on my tummy
down hills of snow,

I would be
colored snow-white,

I would leap across every
gap in the ice,

I would watch
the beautiful sky at night,

I would feast for hours
on freshly caught fish,

and if ever I became
too cold or wet,

I would quickly
turn back into a cat again.

DUDLEY IN A JAM

It was not a good
season for nuts in
Shadyhanger, but
Dudley thought he
had collected enough
to see him through
the winter. What he
needed now was a
big, fat, juicy plum to
make some nutty
plum jam.

Since Dudley's front
door was blocked by nuts,
his only way out was through the window.

His nose twitched in
anticipation as he set off
toward the woods.

By the stump of an
old oak Dudley found a pile
of acorns.

conceived and illustrated by **Peter Cross**

text by **Judy Taylor**

"It's silly to leave these for someone else," he thought, as he munched his way through them all.

A little farther on he came to the plum tree—and there on the ground was the very last plum.

"Buzz off!" said Dudley, flicking away a hungry wasp.

When he returned home, Dudley dropped the plum through the window.

Then he started in after it, but Dudley had eaten too many acorns. He couldn't go forward and he couldn't go backward. He was completely and definitely stuck.

From a long way behind
him, Dudley heard an angry
buzzzZZZZZZZZZZZZZ
ZZZZzzzzzz

The sting gave him such
a shock that he popped
through the window like
a cork from a bottle.

Dudley landed *splat!*
right in the middle of
the ripe plum.

Although the
plum was badly
squashed, it
would still make
good jam.

Dudley put what was left into his special jam-making machine and turned it on.

Dudley stirred and stirred until his eyelids felt heavy. The smell of the new plum jam was delicious.

And Dudley settled down for his long winter sleep before the jam had even begun to cool.

YOU'RE A GENIUS,
BLACKBOARD BEAR

MARTHA ALEXANDER

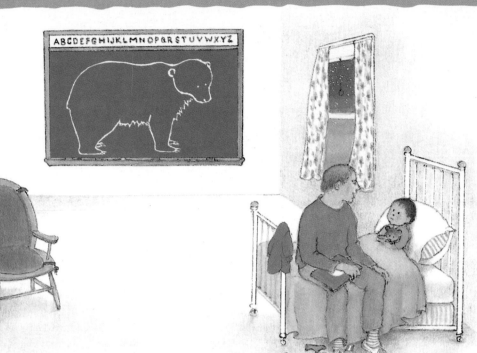

The moon sounds great! Can we go there, Dad?
But, Anthony, I don't know how to build a spaceship.

What are you doing,
Blackboard Bear?
It's the middle of the night.

A spaceship? Really?
You're drawing the parts? Wow!

Oh, I see. You're going to
put it together outside.
Can I help?

WE DID IT! You're a genius!

Do we need to go right away?
What if we get lost?

Oh, you drew a compass to
show us how to get there.

It looks like the moon is all
covered with snow.
I'd better get my snowsuit and
mittens and sleeping bag.

I hope the moon isn't too bumpy.
I bet there's no water up there.
And there's probably nothing
to eat either.

Do you think there are any
monsters on the moon?

You don't really know?
Oh, . . . well . . . it looks like
there's no room for me.
I guess I won't be able to go.

You'll go alone and see what it's
like on the moon?
You wouldn't be afraid without me?
Be careful now.
Don't bump into any stars.

THE DOG and THE BONE

retold by Margaret Clark

illustrated by Charlotte Voake

A dog was walking over a bridge carrying a large bone in her mouth. Looking down into the stream, she saw another dog there. It was carrying an even bigger bone in its mouth. Immediately, the dog on the bridge jumped into the water, snatching for the bigger bone and dropping her own. And then there was just one cold, wet dog and no bone at all!

Dear Mr. Blueberry

Simon James

Dear Mr. Blueberry,

I love whales very much and I think I saw one in my pond today. Please send me some information on whales, as I think he might be hurt.

Love
Emily

Dear Emily,

Here are some details about whales. I don't think you'll find it was a whale you saw, because whales don't live in ponds, but in salt water.

Yours sincerely,
Your teacher,

Mr. Blueberry

Dear Mr. Blueberry,

I am now putting salt into the pond every day before breakfast and last night I saw my whale smile. I think he is feeling better.

Do you think he might be lost?

Love
Emily

Dear Emily,

Please don't put any more salt in the pond. I'm sure your parents won't be pleased.

I'm afraid there can't be a whale in your pond, because whales don't get lost, they always know where they are in the oceans.

Yours sincerely,

Mr. Blueberry

Dear Mr. Blueberry,

Tonight I am very happy because I saw my whale jump up and spurt lots of water. He looked blue.

Does this mean he might be a blue whale?

Love
Emily

PS What can I feed him with?

Dear Emily,

Blue whales are blue and they eat tiny shrimplike creatures that live in the sea. However, I must tell you that a blue whale is much too big to live in your pond.

Yours sincerely,

Mr. Blueberry

PS   Perhaps it is a blue goldfish?

Dear Mr. Blueberry,

Last night I read your letter to my whale. Afterward he let me stroke his head. It was very exciting.

I secretly took him some crunched-up cornflakes and bread crumbs. This morning I looked in the pond and they were all gone!

I think I shall call him Arthur. What do you think?

Love
Emily

Dear Emily,

I must point out to you quite forcibly now that in no way could a whale live in your pond. You may not know that whales are migratory, which means they travel great distances each day.

I am sorry to disappoint you.

Yours sincerely,

Mr. Blueberry

Dear Mr. Blueberry,

Tonight I'm a little sad. Arthur has gone. I think your letter made sense to him and he has decided to be migratory again.

Love
Emily

Dear Emily,

Please don't be too sad, it really was impossible for a whale to live in your pond. Perhaps when you are older you would like to sail the oceans studying and protecting whales.

Yours sincerely,

Mr. Blueberry

Dear Mr. Blueberry,

It's been the happiest day! I went to the beach and you'll never guess, but I saw Arthur! I called to him and he smiled. I knew it was Arthur because he let me stroke his head.
I gave him some of my sandwich . . .

and then we said good-bye. I shouted that I loved him very much and, I hope you don't mind, I said you loved him, too.

Love
Emily (and Arthur)

89

OWL BABIES

Once there were three baby owls:
Sarah and Percy and Bill. They
lived in a hole in the trunk of a
tree with their Owl Mother. The
hole had twigs and leaves and owl
feathers in it. It was their house.

One night they woke up and their
Owl Mother was GONE.
"Where's Mommy?" asked Sarah.
"Oh, my goodness!" said Percy.
"I want my mommy!" said Bill.

The baby owls *thought*
(all owls think a lot)—
"I think she's gone hunting,"
said Sarah.
"To get us our food!" said Percy.
"I want my mommy!" said Bill.

But their Owl Mother didn't come.
The baby owls came out of their
house, and they sat on the tree and
waited.

There was a big branch for Sarah,
a small branch for Percy, and an
old piece of ivy for Bill.
"She'll be back," said Sarah.
"Back *soon*!" said Percy.
"I want my mommy!" said Bill.

It was dark in the woods and they
had to be brave, for things *moved*
all around them.

90

Martin Waddell

illustrated by Patrick Benson

"She'll bring us mice and things that are nice," said Sarah.
"I suppose so!" said Percy.
"I want my mommy!" said Bill.

They sat and they thought (all owls think a lot)—
"I think we should *all* sit on *my* branch," said Sarah.

And they did, all three together.

"Suppose she got lost," said Sarah.
"Or a fox got her!" said Percy.
"I want my mommy!" said Bill.
And the baby owls closed their owl eyes and wished their Owl Mother would come.

AND SHE CAME.
Soft and silent, she swooped
through the trees to Sarah
and Percy and Bill.

"Mommy!" they cried, and they
flapped and they danced, and
they bounced up and down on
their branch.

"WHAT'S ALL THE FUSS?" their
Owl Mother asked.
"You knew I'd come back."

The baby owls thought (all
owls think a lot)—
"I knew it," said Sarah.
"And I knew it!" said Percy.
"I love my mommy!" said Bill.

DATE			
APR 5 199			
APR 25			
MAY 14 199			
MAY 17 199			
MAY 27 199			
JE 7 '97			
JUN 17			